To Patrick — S.McB.
For Kaaren and Paul — P.H.

Published simultaneously in Canada.
First published in the United States 2001 by G. P. Putnam's Sons.
Published in Great Britain 1999 by Macdonald Young Books,
an imprint of Hodder Headline, Limited, UK.

G. P. Putnam's Sons, a division of Penguin Putnam Books
for Young Readers, 345 Hudson Street, New York, NY 10014.
G. P. Putnam's Sons, Reg. U.S. Pat. & Tm. Off.
Printed and bound in Hong Kong
Library of Congress Cataloging-in-Publication Data
McBratney, Sam. Once there was a Hoodie / written by Sam McBratney;
illustrated by Paul Hess. p. cm. Summary: While trying to make
friends, a Hoodie manages to scare off some sheep, cows, and children,
before finding the one thing that will make him truly happy.
[1. Happiness—Fiction.] I. Hess, Paul, ill. II. Title.
PZ7.M47826 On 2001 [E]—dc21 00-023137
ISBN 0-399-23581-7
1 3 5 7 9 10 8 6 4 2
First Impression

ONCE THERE WAS A HOODIE

written by **Sam McBratney**

illustrated by **Paul Hess**

G. P. Putnam's Sons
New York

O nce there was a Hoodie who lived under a hill, and a very fine Hoodie he was.

The Hoodie who lived under the hill wasn't truly happy, for there is only one thing that makes a Hoodie truly happy, and the Hoodie didn't have that.

One day, while out looking for
the one thing that makes a Hoodie truly
happy, the Hoodie saw some white and
woolly creatures in the field below.

He lumbered over to say "Good morning" to them, but the white-and-woollies bolted when they saw him coming.
And they didn't stop running until they had disappeared over the hill.

Funny little beasts, thought the Hoodie. *I hope they don't expect me to chase them.* Hoodies hardly ever hurry, so they're not much good at chasing games.

A few days later
the Hoodie saw
some black and
white creatures
in the field
beyond the fence.

They were chewing grass as busily
as they could chew, and strangely
enough they seemed to be enjoying it.
*I'll say "Good morning" to those
black-and-whites*, thought the Hoodie.

When the black-and-whites saw
the Hoodie coming, they crashed
right through the nearest hedge,
and they didn't stop running
until they had disappeared
over the hill.

Funny creatures, thought the Hoodie.
Maybe they wanted me to chase them, too.

The long days of summer went by. One lazy afternoon as the Hoodie lay out on his hill, he heard voices in the distance. Many tiny two-legged things were coming into his field. The many tiny-two-legs made an amazing amount of noise. Most of them sat down to eat; the others kicked a big black and white roly-poly from one to another.

That looks like a lot of fun, thought the Hoodie.

The Hoodie lumbered down the hill, caught the big black and white roly-poly...

and kicked it out of sight!

Then he noticed
something strange. The many
tiny-two-legs were running away
from him, all waving their arms about
and making more noise than ever.

"Ho-ho," cried the Hoodie, "I'm
sure they want me to chase them!"

He did his best to chase them, but they rushed into a thing that belched out smoke as it disappeared into the distance.

Why do they all want me to play chasing? thought the Hoodie as he returned to his hill.

The summer was almost
over when the Hoodie went
to pick flowers at the edge of
the wood. As he picked the flowers,
the Hoodie paused and sniffed the air.
A beautiful smell was on the breeze.
Could it be the wild rose?
No! This smell was
even more delightful
than the flowers of the field.

Could it be...?

The Hoodie turned around.
He looked once, he looked twice
to make sure that he could really
believe his eyes, and *yes indeed*
—lumbering toward him was the
one thing that makes a Hoodie
truly happy.
It was...

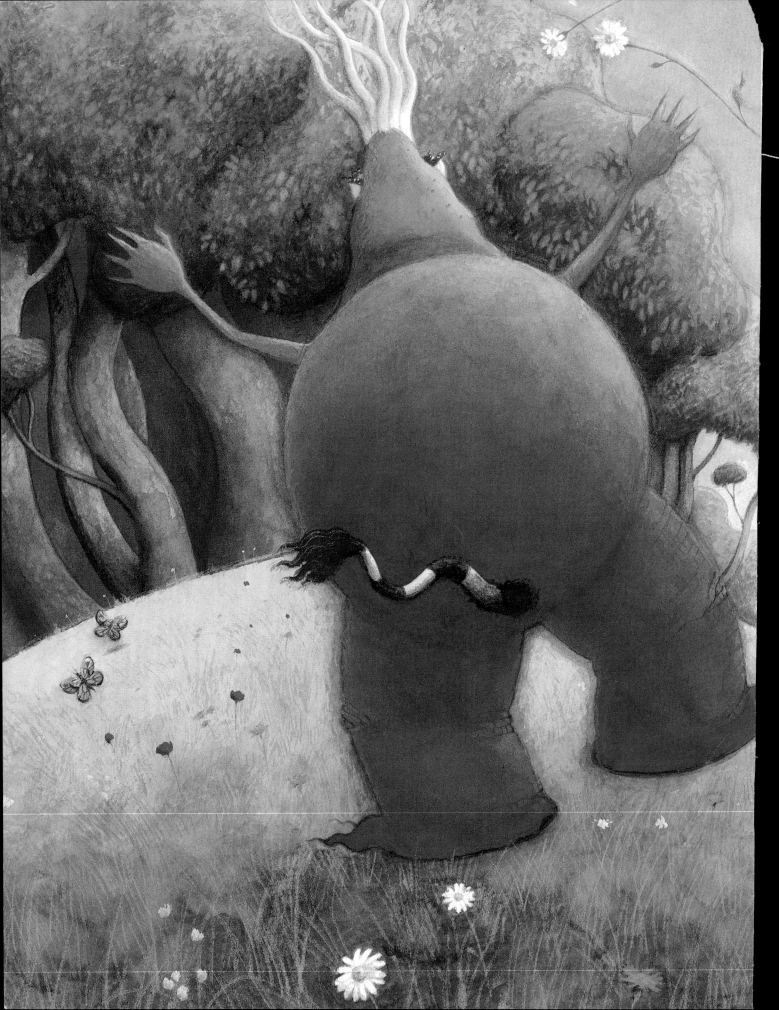

another Hoodie!

This other Hoodie was everything a Hoodie should be. A Hoodie should be as brightly colored as a berry, and this Hoodie was so brightly colored that you could almost call her "dazzling."

Her ears sprouted out from her head the way fungus sprouts out from a tree. She was a very fine Hoodie indeed.

One happy Hoodie hugging another happy Hoodie is a sight to see. They danced among the daisies, they twirled among the trees.

Then the two happy Hoodies lumbered back to the hill, where they had much to talk about before they went to sleep for a hundred years.

And if nothing has happened to the Hoodies since, they must be slumbering still —deep under their hill.

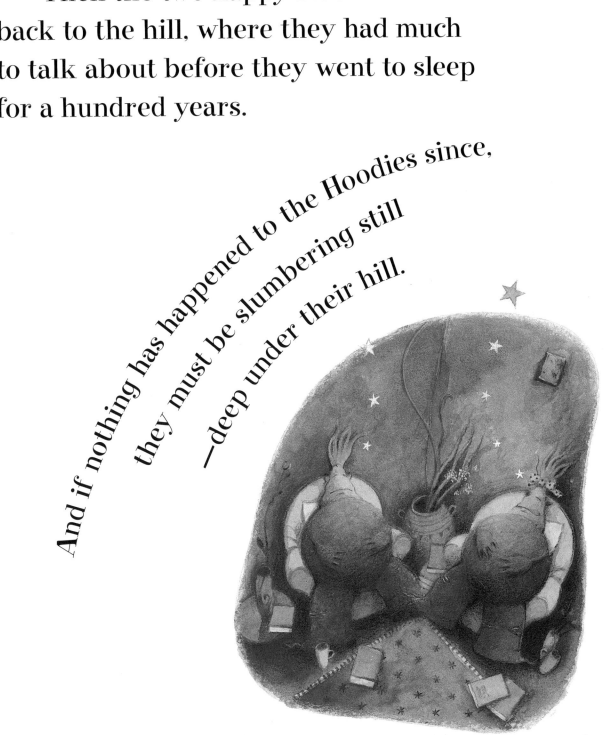